Special thanks to Linda Chapman

For Secret Kingdom readers everywhere

ORCHARD BOOKS

First published in Great Britain in 2015 by Orchard Books
This edition published in 2017 by The Watts Publishing Group

3 5 7 9 10 8 6 4

A CIP catalogue record for this book is available from the British Library.

ISBN 978 1 40834 038 7

Printed in Great Britain by Clays Ltd, St Ives plc

The paper and board used in this book are made from wood from responsible sources

Orchard Books
An imprint of Hachette Children's Group
Part of The Watts Publishing Group Limited
Carmelite House, 50 Victoria Embankment, London EC4Y 0DZ

An Hachette UK Company
www.hachette.co.uk
www.hachettechildrens.co.uk

Series created by Hothouse Fiction
www.hothousefiction.com

Royal
Bridesmaids

ROSIE BANKS

This is the Secret Kingdom

Snow Chateau

The Bride's Surprise

Contents

A Special Invitation

"Would anyone like a chocolate chip cookie?" Mrs Macdonald called up the stairs.

Ellie and her best friends, Summer and Jasmine, jumped to their feet. They were playing snap in Ellie's bedroom but they weren't going to turn down one of Ellie's mum's freshly-baked biscuits.

"Race you downstairs!" Ellie said.

They all charged downstairs and burst into the kitchen. Molly, Ellie's little sister, was sitting at the kitchen table with a cookie in her hand, looking through some old photo albums. With her curly red hair, freckles and green eyes, she looked just like a mini version of Ellie.

"Help yourselves, girls," said Mrs Macdonald, offering a plate of cookies.

"Yum! Thank you!" said Summer, as she bit into a still-warm cookie.

"You make the best cookies, Mrs Macdonald," Jasmine said.

Mrs Macdonald smiled. "Thanks, Jasmine."

"What are you doing, Molly?" Ellie asked, going over to her sister.

"I've got to take some photos into

school," said Molly. "We're doing a project about our families. I've got to take some pictures in of you and Mum and Dad and some of me when I was a baby."

Ellie giggled at the picture of her parents' wedding. "Look at Dad's hair!" It was spiky on top and long at the back. "I'm glad he doesn't look like that any more."

Her mum grinned back. "Me too! But it was stylish at the time."

"I love weddings," said Summer with a sigh, looking at the photos over Ellie's shoulder. Ellie's mum was wearing a white lace wedding dress in the photos and a headdress made of flowers. "Your dress was really beautiful."

"I made it myself," Ellie's mum said.

"We didn't have much money so I made my dress and the bridesmaids' dresses and the cake. We had a wonderful day."

"Did you have dancing after the wedding?" Jasmine asked. She loved dancing.

"We did," said Mrs Macdonald. "We danced all night." Her eyes glowed as she remembered it. "It was so much fun."

"I wish I could go to a wedding," said Ellie. "I've never been to one."

"I was a bridesmaid once but I was too little to remember it," said Jasmine.

"Imagine if we could all go to a wedding and be bridesmaids together," said Summer.

Molly turned the pages of the photo album. "Look at Ellie!"

The girls all giggled. It was a picture

of Ellie as a baby. She was lying on a
changing mat with just a nappy on. She
had no hair, huge green eyes and chubby
legs and arms. "I was a really roly-poly
baby!" Ellie said.

"You were the cutest baby in the
world," her mum said fondly.

"What about me?" Molly said
indignantly.

"OK, you were *both* the cutest babies
in the world," said Mrs Macdonald. "Let's
find some pictures of you now, Molly."

"I can't believe I looked like that when
I was a baby," said Ellie as they went
back upstairs to her room. "My tummy
was almost as tubby as King Merry's!"

"No one's tummy could be as round as
King Merry's," said Summer.

King Merry was the ruler of the Secret

Kingdom, a magical land that only Ellie, Summer and Jasmine knew about. They had been there lots of times and met all sorts of amazing people and creatures – tiny pixies and giant dream dragons, beautiful unicorns and cuddly snow bears.

"It's been ages since we last went to the Secret Kingdom," said Jasmine. "Let's check the Magic Box. There might be a message for us."

Whenever King Merry wanted the girls to come to the Secret Kingdom, a riddle appeared in the Magic Box's mirrored lid.

Ellie knelt down on the floor. There were two big wicker baskets under her bed and she started to pull one out. "I put the Magic Box in here to keep it—" She broke off with a gasp as sparkling light flooded out.

"The Magic Box is glowing!" said Summer.

"There must be a message! Quick, Ellie!" said Jasmine.

Ellie took the Magic Box out of the basket. A riddle was scrolling across its lid. Her heart raced as she read out the words:

"Where parties are held and sweet
bubbles fly,
King Merry awaits where pink turrets
reach high!"

The lid of the box opened and a large
map of the Secret Kingdom floated out,
but the girls didn't need its help this time.

"The answer to that riddle is obvious,"
said Jasmine. "It's got to be King Merry's
Enchanted Palace."

Ellie nodded. "King Merry has lots of
parties there and it's got beautiful pink
turrets."

"And a bubbly lemonade fountain in
the garden!" said Summer. "Come on!"
She put her hands on the beautifully
carved box.

The others copied her and then they all said together: "The Enchanted Palace!"

WHOOSH! A sparkling ball of green light shot out of the Magic Box. It zoomed round the girls' heads then transformed into a tiny pixie standing on a green leaf. "Hello, girls!" she said, smiling. Her blonde hair was tucked under a cap made of green leaves, and she was wearing a dress made of daisies.

"Trixi!" the girls cried.

"It's lovely to see you all!" said Trixi.

"What's happening, Trixi?" said Jasmine. "Is there a problem in the Secret Kingdom?"

"No, not at all," said Trixi. "King Merry just wants you to come and meet one of his relatives."

"Not Queen Malice?" Ellie said, alarmed. Queen Malice was the king's horrible sister. She wanted to rule the Secret Kingdom and make it a miserable, unhappy place. She was always hatching nasty plots.

Trixi grinned. "No, don't worry. This relative of the king's is MUCH nicer. She's the king's cousin, Lady Felicity. Would you like to come and meet her?"

"Definitely!" Jasmine, Ellie and Summer exclaimed happily.

They held hands and Trixi tapped the green ring on her finger:

"To the palace, please, my magic ring,
Whisk us there, to see the king!"

A cloud of sparkles burst out of the ring and swirled round the girls. Gasping with delight, they felt themselves being lifted into the air and whisked away!

An Unwanted Guest

"We're back in the Secret Kingdom!"
Summer said. Excitement fizzed inside
her as the sparkles faded and she saw
that the magic had brought them to the
palace gardens. She touched her head
and felt the tiara that was now nestling
in her blonde hair. The tiaras always
appeared when the girls arrived in the

Secret Kingdom. They showed everyone in the land that they were Very Important Friends of King Merry.

"It looks just as wonderful as ever!" said Ellie, her green eyes shining as she looked around.

The lemonade fountain was shooting bubbles into the air and butterflies fluttered around amongst the banks of brightly coloured flowers.

"And look! There's King Merry!" said Jasmine as the ballroom doors opened and a small, smiling figure came out.

As always, his crown was slipping sideways on his white curls and his half-moon spectacles were halfway down his nose. "Oh, crowns and coronations! My friends are here!" he cried, opening his arms wide. "It's so good to see you."

The girls ran up the steps and gave him a big hug.

"I can't wait for you to meet my cousin," King Merry said, straightening his crown. "Her wedding to Prince Noel is tomorrow and it is going to be a day full of love, laughter and magic. You are all invited."

The girls swapped excited looks.

"We were just talking about weddings and saying how much we would like to go to one," said Summer.

"Well, now you shall!" King Merry said. "This wedding will be very special. We have a saying here in the Secret Kingdom:

"*When a prince from the north takes a southern lady for his bride, the kingdom's love and magic will spread far and wide!*

"My cousin is from the sunny south of the kingdom and the prince lives at the Snow Chateau in the north, so when they get married the Secret Kingdom will become an even more magical and happy place – love will sweep over the whole land!"

Summer sighed. "That's so romantic!"

"I know!" said King Merry in delight. "But that's not until tomorrow. Today is my cousin's bridal shower – a party given by her family and friends. Do come into the palace and meet everyone."

The girls and Trixi followed the king through the doors into a huge hallway with a spiral staircase in the centre.

A young lady was coming down the stairs. She wore a long pink-and-gold dress and had a golden tiara in her dark

hair. Her blue eyes were just as kind and
sparkling as King Merry's.

"Lady Felicity,
my dear. These
are my
friends Ellie,
Summer and
Jasmine," said
King Merry.

"How
wonderful to
meet you
all." Lady
Felicity

smiled at the girls. "I've heard so much
about you." It was impossible not to smile
back. Lady Felicity seemed to radiate
happiness and light.

"It's lovely to meet you too, Lady

Felicity," said Jasmine.

"Is Prince Noel here?" asked Ellie.

"No, he's getting the Snow Chateau ready for the wedding," said Lady Felicity. "After lunch, King Merry and I shall set off for the north."

As she spoke there was the sound of bells ringing. The peal of bells finished with four loud bongs.

"What are those bells for?" Ellie asked curiously.

"They are counting down the hours until Lady Felicity and I must leave," said King Merry. "They will ring throughout the land every hour until we depart so that people will know when to line the roads and cheer. Everyone wants to see Lady Felicity to wish her luck and love."

Bobbins, King Merry's head butler,

came up to King Merry and cleared
his throat. "Your majesty, the guests are
waiting."

King Merry beamed. "Then let
us join them. Come, my
dears!"

Bobbins opened
a door to a
sun-filled
room
with huge
windows that
looked on
to the garden.
Garlands of pink
roses decorated the
walls, and rose petals covered
the floor. There was a long table covered
with delicious-looking food and guests

were drinking fruit punch from dainty
crystal glasses.

When the king and Lady Felicity
walked in with the girls and Trixi, the
guests started to bow and
curtsey.

"Oh, please my
friends, there
is no need
for that,"
said King
Merry. "Now,
cousin," he
said, turning
to Lady Felicity.
"Would you like
to take your seat so we can start the
ceremony?"

"Of course." Lady Felicity smiled and

sat on a golden chair.

"What's happening?" Summer whispered to Trixi.

"There's a special tradition here in the Secret Kingdom," Trixi explained. "The bride is given four magical gifts by her friends and family:

"*Something precious, something shiny, something gold, something tiny.*

"If Lady Felicity wears them on her wedding day they'll bring her good luck throughout her married life."

Ellie smiled. "We do something similar in our world. The bride wears something old, something new, something borrowed and something blue when she gets married."

"Only the things aren't magic," said Summer. "I wish they were, though!"

Bobbins blew a fanfare on a trumpet.
The door opened and in came four other
elf butlers. Each was carrying a small
pink cushion on which perched an object.

"Oh, sceptres and spells, this is so much
fun!" said King
Merry, his crown
wobbling as he
did a happy
little jig on the
spot. Then he
presented Lady
Felicity with
the first gift. "Lady
Felicity, here is something
very precious – a comb that my mother
wore on her own wedding day."

The comb was golden and decorated
with gems.

"That's so pretty," Ellie whispered to her friends.

King Merry moved to the second cushion and picked up a small ring with a heart-shaped pink stone. "And here is something tiny, but full of magic."

"Gorgeous," murmured Jasmine, as Lady Felicity admired the ring.

The little king moved to the third gift. "And here is something to bring you lots of luck: a golden horseshoe."

"How lovely," Summer said.

Finally, King Merry picked up the fourth gift, which sparkled in the sunlight. "And last but not least, a shiny emerald necklace. They are all for you, my dear, with our love and best wishes!"

Beaming, Lady Felicity clasped her hands together and opened her mouth to speak but before she could say anything there was a loud rumble of thunder. The skies outside darkened. Everyone looked around in surprise.

"What's happening?' said one of the guests.

Summer's stomach curled anxiously. Thunder in the Secret Kingdom usually meant just one thing… "Oh no," she whispered to Jasmine and Ellie. "You don't think it's Queen Malice, do you?"

The girls grabbed each other's hands as a horribly familiar cackling filled the room!

Something Old

Queen Malice appeared on top of the food table, her black boots trampling the pretty cakes. Her eyes glittered like jet on either side of her pointy nose. "So, you thought you'd have a family wedding without inviting me, did you, brother?" she said, glaring at King Merry. "Well, I shall ruin your little celebration!"

She jumped down from the table and swung her thunderstaff in a circle around the room. The guests shrank back with gasps of alarm.

"Sister, please," said King Merry, wringing his hands. "There's no need for any trouble. Of course you can come to the wedding. But you will have to promise to be nice."

"Never!" hissed the queen.

"You must. This is a very important wedding. It will make the Secret Kingdom even more magical," said King Merry.

"Not if I can help it!" snarled Queen Malice. She stalked towards where the four elves were holding the wedding gifts. "Hmm. What have we got here? Ah, yes. *Something precious, something shiny, something gold, something tiny.* All to bring good luck. Well, not any more!" She called out a curse:

"Change these gifts from good to bad,
Make the wedding drab and sad!"

Before anyone could stop her, four lightning bolts flew from her staff and hit each of the cushions. There was a bang, and smoke drifted up from the cushions.

As it cleared everyone saw that the gifts had changed – the tiny ring had become a puddle of slime, the precious comb had become an old boot, the shiny necklace had changed into a stink toad and the golden horseshoe had become a lump of dirty ice.

Jasmine gasped. "What have you done, Queen Malice?"

"Look at what you have now," Queen Malice hissed at Lady Felicity, who was trembling. "*Something slimy, something old, something smelly, something cold* – to bring BAD luck. I hope you enjoy your miserable wedding tomorrow. I didn't want to come anyway!"

She gave a shriek of mean laughter and disappeared.

The stink toad hopped off the cushion with a loud croak. A horrible smell drifted from its knobbly skin.

"Go away! Shoo!" said King Merry flapping his hands at it. "Oh, dear, this is a disaster!"

Trying not to breathe in the smell, Summer picked the toad up. Ellie opened the window and Summer let it hop down on to the grass.

"Oh, cousin, what is going to happen?" cried Lady Felicity, tears trickling down her cheeks. "I won't have good luck and happiness now."

"Maybe we can help," said Jasmine. "If Trixi helps us, we could use her magic to travel round the kingdom quickly and find some new gifts for Lady Felicity."

"Of course I'll help," said Trixi. "I can't believe Queen Malice did something so horrid."

"I can," said Summer.

Ellie nodded. "She always wants to spoil
things but we won't let her ruin your
wedding," she told Lady Felicity.

Lady Felicity smiled through her tears.
"Thank you. You're all so kind."

"My friends have never let me down
before," said King Merry.

"And we won't let you down now,"
said Jasmine determinedly. She turned to
the others. "First of all we need to find a
precious hair comb. Where can we find
something like that?"

"Who uses hair combs?" said Trixi.
"Um, let's see…"

"Mermaids!" said Ellie suddenly.
"Do you remember when we met the
mermaids who live in the Snowy Seas?

Lots of them had combs in their hair."

"Maybe Lady Frida will help us."
Summer pictured the beautiful mermaid
with her sparkling green tail and long
blonde hair.

"Let's go to the Ice Palace and see,"
said Jasmine.

"Do hurry, my dears," said King Merry.
"Lady Felicity and I must leave for the
Snow Chateau in just a few hours."

"We'll be back as quickly as we can,"
promised Summer.

"Hold hands, girls!" Trixi tapped her
ring and called out:

*"To the Ice Palace in the Snowy Seas,
Please clothe us warmly so we won't
freeze!"*

Green sparkles whooshed out and
surrounded the girls. Before they even
had chance to call out goodbye, they
were whisked away.

They felt the cold air on their faces
as the sparkles had cleared. But their
bodies and feet felt toasty warm. Summer
saw they were all wearing ski outfits,
fur-lined boots, hats and gloves. Even
Trixi was wearing a tiny ski outfit with a
bobble hat.

"Oh, wow!" said Jasmine. "I like our clothes."

Trixi swooped round them on her leaf. "Good!" she said, smiling. "They should keep us snug and warm."

"Look at the palace!" said Summer. It was as beautiful as she remembered – with towering turrets and walls made of glittering ice decorated with carvings of starfish.

"Last time we came here we turned into mermaids," remembered Ellie.

"That was fun but I'm afraid we haven't got time for that now," said Trixi. "We must get back as quickly as we can."

Jasmine ran to the front door and banged the fish-shaped knocker.

The door swung open by magic. The girls hurried inside and found themselves in a big hall in which was a huge swimming pool lined with silver tiles. One wall had a large window that looked out over the sparkling blue sea and ice floes. Merpeople were swimming in the pool's water and brightly coloured pingaloos waddled around the edges of the pool, squawking to each other.

Four merpeople were clustered around a block of ice, carving it into the shape of a bride and a groom. Nearby, a beautiful mermaid with long blonde hair and a green tail was sitting on a silver throne, giving instructions to the sculptors. Her eyes lit up when she saw her visitors.

"My friends, what a lovely surprise!"

"*Pingalooooo!*" The penguin-like birds squawked as they recognised their friends and waddled over to them.

The girls stroked the pingaloos' heads before approaching Lady Frida.

"Hello, Lady Frida," called Jasmine. "We've come from the Enchanted Palace."

"We really need your help," said Summer.

"Queen Malice is causing trouble again," said Ellie. "Did you know that Lady Felicity is about to marry Prince Noel?"

"Of course. My ice carvers are sculpting a special statue to mark the occasion," said Lady Frida, pointing at the ice figures of the bride and groom.

"Well, Queen Malice is trying to ruin the wedding," said Ellie. She told Lady Frida how Queen Malice had changed the bride's gifts into horrible objects.

"We need to find some replacement gifts that will bring good luck," said Ellie.

"We wondered if you might have a precious comb that could replace the one that belonged to King Merry's mother," said Trixi.

Lady Frida smiled. "I have just the thing!" She pulled a silver comb out of her blonde hair. It was shaped like a shell and decorated with pearls. "This comb is full of mermaid magic. I would be honoured if Lady Felicity wears it on her wedding day."

"Oh, thank you so much!" said Jasmine taking the comb. She wound her long hair into a bun and used the comb to hold it in place.

"Lady Felicity and King Merry will both be so happy with this," said Ellie in delight.

Lady Frida smiled. "Good. It's always my pleasure to help the king and his family."

"If we can find the other three gifts as quickly as this then we might just make it back in time," said Jasmine.

"What else do you need to get?" Lady Frida asked.

"Something gold, something shiny, and something tiny," said Summer.

Trixi turned a loop-the-loop. "Ooh! I've just had an idea of where we can get something tiny! Why don't we see if my Aunt Maybelle can help? She might have a pixie ring that Lady Felicity can have."

"Brilliant idea, Trixi!" said Jasmine.

As she spoke there was a peal of bells. It ended with three loud bongs.

"Oh, goodness! We've only got three hours left now!" said Summer.

"Goodbye, my friends. Please give all our love to Lady Felicity," said Lady Frida. "And tell her we would be delighted to show her and Prince Noel the ice sculpture."

"We'll tell them," promised Ellie.

"Goodbye!" they all called as they held hands.

Trixi tapped her ring and called out a spell:

"To the school where pixies fly,
On magic leaves, way up high!"

"Here we go again!" cried Ellie as they were swept away.

Something Tiny

The girls landed on something soft, green
and bouncy – it felt like a giant squashy
cushion.

Jasmine opened her eyes and squealed
as she saw they were now the same size
as Trixi. "Trixi! You've made us pixie-
sized, and we're on your leaf!"

Trixi giggled. "I had to make my leaf
bigger to carry us all, though."

Ellie gulped as
she peeked over
the edge of
the leaf and
saw that they
were whizzing
over a wood.
"We're very high
up," she quavered.

She didn't like heights and they were
travelling fast.

"Don't worry," said Trixi. "We'll be
there soon. Look, there's the Flying
School." She pointed down through the
trees.

The girls caught their breath as the
leaf swooped down towards a glittering
white castle standing in a glade. Purple
flags embroidered with gold pixie leaves

flew from the turrets and the four walls
surrounded a square of green grass.
Pixies were flying around the square on
different shaped leaves. They were flying
in pairs then meeting in the middle,
swooping up and down and turning
loop-the-loops.

"Everyone's practising their routine
for the wedding display,"
said Trixi. "There's Aunt
Maybelle teaching
them!"

The girls saw a familiar grey-haired figure standing in the centre of the grassy square. Trixi's Aunt Maybelle had once been headmistress of the Flying School. She was retired now and lived in a little cottage near the school but she still came and taught the pupils on special occasions. She was calling out instructions, magically magnifying her voice, so it sounded as if she was using a megaphone.

"And flying high…double flip and back to the centre. Excellent work, everyone!"

"Aunt Maybelle!" Trixi cried as her leaf landed.

"Why, Trixi, my dear," said Aunt Maybelle, blinking in surprise as Trixi and the girls jumped off. "Whatever brings you all here?" Her eyes widened anxiously. "Is something wrong at the palace?"

"It is, I'm afraid," said Jasmine. She explained what had happened.

"Queen Malice is dreadful!" said Aunt Maybelle when Jasmine had finished. "Right, we must sort this out. I'm sure I can help."

She tapped her pixie ring and her voice was loud and clear when she called out, "Pixies, please carry on practising while I attend to some business. I look forward to seeing some perfect triple flips when I come back." She turned to the girls. "Now, come with me."

She led the way out of the castle gates and down the path. Aunt Maybelle's cottage was at the edge of the glade, nestled among the roots of an oak tree. It had a thatched roof, a wishing well in the garden and pink roses covering the walls. Aunt Maybelle opened the door and they all went inside. They followed Aunt Maybelle into her bedroom where there was a bed covered with a beautiful patchwork quilt.

Aunt Maybelle took a jewellery box

off her dressing table. "Now, where is it?"
She rummaged around
for a while, and then
took out a gold ring
that had little ruby
hearts embedded in
the band. "This was
my grandmother's
ring. Lady Felicity
can have it as her
wedding ring."

"Oh, thank you, Aunt Maybelle," said
Summer. It was so beautiful and delicate.
"I bet Lady Felicity will love it."

"Wait," said Ellie as Summer was
about to slip the ring into her pocket.
"We need something tiny, but that ring
will be much too small for Lady Felicity
to wear."

"Of course," said Jasmine, realising Ellie was right. "We need a human-sized ring."

"We'll have to find it somewhere else," Summer said anxiously. As she spoke there was another peal of bells and two bongs rang out. "There are only two hours left now! Time's whizzing by. What are we going to do?"

"Wait, wait! It's OK. I can change the size of the ring with my magic!" said Trixi. She tapped her own pixie ring:

*"Aunt Maybelle's gift is just the thing,
But please grow bigger, magic ring."*

There was a flash and the wedding ring grew bigger.

"Now it will fit Lady Felicity," said Trixi. She took the ring from Summer

and slipped it over her
head like a necklace.
"I'll keep it safe."

"Does it still count
as *something tiny*?"
asked Summer.

"Of course," said
Trixi. "King Merry's
something tiny was a ring,
too."

Aunt Maybelle smiled. "Well done, my
dear. Now, hurry to find the last two
gifts."

"Something gold and something shiny,"
said Ellie.

"The gold object must be a horseshoe,"
said Trixi. "Brides in the Secret Kingdom
always carry a golden horseshoe for
good luck."

"Maybe we can ask the unicorns?" suggested Ellie. "They've always helped us in the past."

"Ah, but unicorns don't wear horseshoes," said Aunt Maybelle.

The girls thought hard. What horses had they met in the Secret Kingdom?

"I know!" said Summer. "Do you remember the flying horses from Sparkle Slopes? We helped them escape from some horrible trolls."

Ellie nodded. "The trolls were making them pick all the diamonds that grow on the trees there for Queen Malice."

"The leader was called Swift," added Jasmine.

"Go to see them, my dears," said Aunt Maybelle. "I am sure they will help you."

"I hope the trolls don't come back,"

said Trixi with a shiver.

Jasmine lifted her chin. "So what if they do? We won't let a troll stop us from helping Lady Felicity!"

Summer grabbed her friends' hands. "To the Sparkle Slopes!" she said.

Something Gold

Trixi tapped her ring and called out another spell:

*"Now to the slopes of sparkly snow,
Where horses fly and diamonds grow!"*

When they landed halfway up a snow-covered mountain, the girls were back to their normal size. It was very cold on the

Snowy Slopes and they were glad to find that they were wearing their pretty ski-suits again.

"I'd forgotten how beautiful the Snowy Slopes are," said Summer. "Look at all the diamonds on the trees!"

Sure enough, diamonds of all shapes and sizes grew on the branches of the trees. They sent out a dazzling light.

Suddenly, a shadow passed by overhead. They all looked up in alarm. But to their relief

it was a beautiful white
horse with sparkling wings
and a long mane and tail. He was
swooping through the sky.

"Swift!" shouted Jasmine, waving madly.

The others joined in. "Swift! Over
here!"

The horse gave a delighted whinny
and flew down to meet them. He landed
lightly on the snow.

"Hello, my friends. It's lovely to see you
again." He nuzzled the girls with his nose.
"What are you all doing here?"

"We came here to find you, Swift," said Summer, stroking his silky mane. "We were hoping you might help us."

"Do you think we could have one of your horseshoes...?" Ellie broke off as she looked at Swift's hooves. She saw Summer and Jasmine's faces fall as they followed her gaze. "Oh, but your shoes are silver, not gold."

"We need a gold horseshoe for Lady Felicity," Jasmine explained, her heart sinking. "We'll have to go somewhere else."

"No you won't," Swift whinnied. "My shoes *are* made of gold. They're made of white gold, it just looks like silver!"

The girls breathed sighs of relief.

"I can't give you one of my shoes because I need them to stop myself from slipping in the snow," said Swift. "But I can fly you down the mountain to where the fairy goldsmiths live. They make my shoes and I'm sure they will be happy to give you a golden horseshoe for Lady Felicity."

"That would be wonderful! Thank you!" said Summer, giving him a hug.

Just then the girls heard a peal of bells, ending with one loud bong.

"We've only got one hour left! Quick!" said Jasmine.

Swift knelt down so they could all climb on to his back. Trixi flew on her leaf beside Swift as he spread his wings out and soared up into the air. The girls' hair blew out behind them and the frosty air stung their cheeks. If they hadn't been so worried about getting back to the

palace in time they would have loved it –
even Ellie.

Swift landed just outside a cave at the
bottom of the slope. It had a red door
and light was shining out from its little
round windows. "Here we are. This is
where the fairy goldsmiths work."

The girls scrambled off Swift's back and
hurried to the door but as they got closer
they realised that it was ajar. There were
bangs and crashes coming from inside.

"What's going on?" said Jasmine. She
ran to one of the windows and gasped.
"Look!"

The cave would have looked very cosy
with its burning fire and work benches
covered with delicate tools and beautiful
golden jewellery – but there were two big
hairy trolls inside. They were swinging

their clubs around, whacking the tables so
the gold necklaces, rings and bracelets fell
on to the floor.

Fairies a bit smaller than the girls were
fluttering around their heads. "Stop!
Please stop!" they cried helplessly.

"No!" shouted the trolls, banging their clubs. "Queen Malice told us to destroy all these stupid wedding gifts!"

Jasmine was too cross to be frightened of the big trolls. She marched to the door and pulled it open wide. "Oh, no you don't!" she said angrily.

Ellie and Summer ran in after her. "You big bullies!" said Ellie.

"Get out of here and leave the poor fairies alone!" said Summer.

The trolls roared in anger when they saw them. "It's those pesky human girls! Get them!" And raising their clubs, they charged straight at the girls!

Something Shiny

The trolls swung their clubs.

"Duck!" yelled Jasmine.

She, Ellie and Summer ducked just in time.

THWACK!

The trolls hit each other instead of the girls.

"Ow!" they exclaimed, falling onto their hairy bottoms. They rubbed their heads.

"That hurt!" one complained.

Jasmine saw that this was their chance. "Get snowballs!" she shouted.

She ran outside and grabbed a handful of snow. Making it into a ball, she threw it hard at the one of the trolls and it hit his head.

"Stop it!" he moaned.

But the girls didn't stop! Ellie and

Summer ran outside and grabbed handfuls of snow. Soon they were pelting the trolls with snowballs too. The fairies and Trixi joined in.

The trolls staggered to their feet. "Leave us alone!" they said, trying to fend the snowballs off.

"No!" shouted Jasmine. "Not until you go away!" Her snowball hit one of the trolls on the nose. SPLAT!

"Scram, trolls!" yelled Ellie, hitting the other troll on his ear.

"Get out of here and don't come back!" cried the fairies.

The trolls roared unhappily and lumbered to the door. As they stumbled outside, Swift, who had been watching from outside, galloped towards them furiously. "How dare you attack the fairies, you great big hairy bullies? Take this!" He kicked up snow with his back hooves, sending it flying in the trolls' ugly faces.

The trolls howled and charged away across the snow, their huge feet leaving big footprints in the snow. Swift chased after them, whinnying angrily.

"Oh, thank you!" cried the fairies, fluttering around the girls. "Thank you so much!" They were dressed in cute little leather aprons and boots.

"You're King Merry's special friends, aren't you?" said a fairy with big brown eyes, golden hair and large, glittering wings.

"We are," said Ellie. "I'm Ellie, this is Jasmine, and this is Summer – and this is Trixi, King Merry's royal pixie."

"Pleased to meet you!" said Trixi.

"I'm Goldie, the head of the fairy goldsmiths," said the fairy. "What brings you here?"

"Queen Malice," said Ellie. All the fairies gathered round and she explained.

"So, you need a golden horseshoe," said Goldie.

"We really do," said Summer.

Goldie spun round. "It will be our

pleasure to make it." She clapped her hands. "Fairies, one horseshoe, if you please."

The fairies all set to work, warming a block of gold in the fire and then quickly hammering it into shape with their tools. They cooled it with a wave of their wands and then made it float up towards the girls.

Summer caught it. It glittered beautifully. "Oh, thank you!" she said. "This is perfect!" She untied the hair ribbon from her ponytail. Tying it onto both ends of the horseshoe, she slipped it over her arm like a bag.

Goldie smiled and said, "Please give our love to the king and to the happy couple."

"Oh, no," gasped Jasmine, catching sight of a golden clock hanging on the wall. "We're running out of time!"

There were only ten minutes left until Lady Felicity and King Merry were due to leave the palace.

"What's the matter?" asked Goldie.

"We still need something shiny that Lady Felicity can wear," explained Ellie. "It's the fourth gift that she needs. We've only got three things so far."

"But we have to get it to her before she leaves for the Snow Chateau," said Summer. "We only have a few minutes!"

Her eyes filled with tears. She couldn't bear the thought that they'd let Lady Felicity down.

"We can help!" said Goldie. "If Swift can pick you some diamonds, we can make it into a necklace. It could replace the wedding gifts that the trolls ruined too."

"Is there time?" asked Ellie.

"If we all work together we should be able to do it really quickly!" said the fairy. "But we'll need someone to design the necklace."

"I can do that!" said Ellie. She loved drawing things and she could already imagine a necklace that would look lovely on Lady Felicity. "I just need some paper."

Two fairies flew over at once with some

paper and a pencil.

"I'll help the fairies tidy up their tools," said Trixi.

"And Summer and I can help Swift find diamonds!" said Jasmine.

"Find a really big one," said Ellie, who was already drawing a heart-shaped setting, "and four little ones too."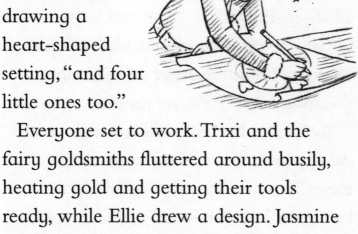

Everyone set to work. Trixi and the fairy goldsmiths fluttered around busily, heating gold and getting their tools ready, while Ellie drew a design. Jasmine and Summer raced outside and explained to Swift what they needed.

"Get on my back," he said. "We'll fly to the diamond trees."

Summer and Jasmine climbed on to Swift's smooth back. Their hearts were beating fast. Would they find the gems in time?

Swift set off into the air, his powerful wings beating. He swooped towards a cluster of trees. There were diamonds on every branch.

"Can we have that one, please? And that one!" said Summer and Jasmine, pointing out the diamonds they wanted.

Swift used his wings to flick the jewels off the branches and the girls caught them.

"We still need a really big one," said Summer, looking round.

"There!" said Jasmine, spotting a large

diamond hidden in the branches. "That one's perfect!"

Swift flicked it with his wings.

"It's pink!" exclaimed Summer as she caught it.

"Pink diamonds are very rare – and especially lucky!" said Swift. "Now let's hurry back to the workshop."

He raced back to the cave. As soon
as he landed, Jasmine and Summer
scrambled off his back. Inside the
workshop, the fairies put the diamonds
in place and then waved their wands.
There was a bright flash of light and
suddenly a necklace was glittering on the
workbench. The sparkling pink diamond
was set in a heart shape with four small
white diamonds set around it.

"We've done it!" cried Ellie, picking the
shining necklace up and slipping it over
her head.

"Quick, we've got to go!" said Trixi,
glancing at the clock. "We may already
be too late."

"Please wish Lady Felicity lots of luck
and love," said Goldie as the girls grabbed
each other's hands.

"We'll tell her this is a special gift from you," said Ellie.

"Goodbye!" whinnied Swift.

"Thank you!" called the girls as Trixi tapped her ring and whisked them away. "And goodbye!"

Just In Time

The magic set them down gently just
outside the Enchanted Palace gates.
A golden coach pulled by four white
unicorns was about to set off. Lady
Felicity and King Merry were sitting
inside it. The girls could see that Lady
Felicity was crying.

"Dearest cousin, please don't cry. Look!
My friends have returned as I said they

would!" King Merry opened the carriage door and jumped down. "Did you manage to find four new gifts?"

Trixi zoomed over to King Merry. "We did, King Merry! We did!" She performed a double loop-the-loop on her leaf that would have made Aunt Maybelle proud.

"Here is a precious comb from the Ice Mermaids," said Jasmine, pulling the comb out her hair and handing it to Lady Felicity who had stepped out of the carriage too. "Lady Frida from the

Snowy Seas sent it with her best wishes.
The Ice Mermaids are making an ice
sculpture in honour of your wedding."

"They would love you to visit them
and see it!" said Summer.

"Oh, I shall!" said Lady Felicity.

"And this is something tiny from my
Aunt Maybelle," said Trixi, pulling the
ring over her head and flying up to give
it to Lady Felicity. "It's a magic pixie
ring. Aunt Maybelle hopes you'll wear it
on your wedding day."

"It's perfect. I will thank her at the
wedding," said Lady Felicity.

"This was made by the fairy
goldsmiths," said Summer, handing Lady
Felicity the horseshoe. "Everyone from
Sparkle Slopes wishes you and Prince
Noel lots of luck tomorrow."

"The fairy goldsmiths also made this diamond necklace," said Ellie. She took it off and held it up. It sparkled in the sunlight. "Our friend Swift helped us find the diamonds."

Lady's Felicity's hands flew to her mouth and happy tears filled her eyes. "It's so beautiful. Oh, girls, you don't know how much all these gifts mean to me. You are wonderful – and Trixi too, of course! Thank you!"

King Merry pulled a spotted

handkerchief out of his cloak and handed it to her. "There, there," he said, as Lady Felicity dabbed at her tears.

Summer smiled. "We're just glad we could help."

The others nodded.

"I would love to hear more about your adventure but we must be on our way," said King Merry, looking at the excited crowd lining the road. "And you must return home, my friends."

"We can come back tomorrow, though, can't we, King Merry?" Summer said. "For the wedding."

"Of course!" he said. "I shall send you a message in the morning."

Lady Felicity beamed at the girls. "I would be honoured if you girls would agree to be my bridesmaids."

Summer, Ellie and Jasmine all squealed in delight.

"Oh, yes, yes, yes!" said Ellie.

"We'd love to!" said Jasmine.

"It would be a dream come true!" said Summer, her eyes shining.

"Then I shall see you tomorrow morning," said Lady Felicity. She got back into the coach, followed by King Merry.

"Goodbye, my friends," he called. "Until tomorrow!"

"Goodbye!" the girls called.

Bobbins blew a fanfare, bells rang out joyously and the unicorns trotted off. King Merry and Lady Felicity waved from the windows and the crowds cheered even louder.

Jasmine, Summer and Ellie waved until

the carriage had disappeared into the distance.

Trixi smiled at them. "I had better send you home now. But look out for a message tomorrow."

"Oh, we will!" promised Summer.

"There's no way we're missing out on the wedding!" said Jasmine.

"And on being bridesmaids," said Ellie with a grin.

Trixi tapped her ring and for the last time that day, sparkles surrounded the girls, carrying them away in a glowing cloud of magic.

They landed back in Ellie's room.

"That was so much fun," said Ellie, breathing out.

"I'm glad we were there to stop Queen Malice," said Summer.

Jasmine frowned. "Do you think she'll do anything tomorrow?"

"I bet she will," said Ellie. "She'll probably try again to ruin the wedding."

"Well, we'll stop her if she does!" Summer said. "Nothing's going to spoil the wedding. Not while we're bridesmaids."

"Nothing at all!" Jasmine and Ellie declared.

Wedding Belles

Contents

❧ A Mysterious Gift ❧

"Here's a bouquet," said Ellie, handing Jasmine a bunch of flowers they had picked in the garden.

"And here's a veil," said Summer, putting an old net curtain over Jasmine's head.

Jasmine had a long skirt of her mum's covering her jeans. The girls were at Jasmine's house for the day. While they were waiting for a message to appear in the Magic Box, they had decided to have a pretend wedding.

Just then Nani, Jasmine's grandmother, came in. "What are you doing, girls?"

"Playing weddings," said Jasmine.

Nani smiled. "I used to do that when I was a girl."

"What was your real wedding like?" Ellie asked her.

"Very different from the weddings in this country," Nani said. "I got married in India, where I grew up. I wore a red-and-gold sari instead of a white dress, we got married outside and celebrated for three days." Nani sighed as she remembered.

"It sounds amazing," said Jasmine.

Nani nodded. "It was. Maybe I can find a few old saris upstairs for you and you can play at having an Indian wedding too."

"Thanks, Nani!" Jasmine said in delight.

Nani left the room. "Should we check the Magic Box while Nani's upstairs?" whispered Ellie.

"Good idea." Jasmine hurried to her bag. "It will probably take Nani a while to find the saris."

She pulled the box out. It wasn't shining at all.

"There's no message yet," said Ellie in disappointment.

Just then Summer saw a spark flash across the lid. "Wait! Look!"

Another flash zipped across the mirror. Suddenly the whole box lit up and words floated across the lid.

"It's King Merry's message!" said Ellie. Summer read it out:

"Come to the north, all covered in snow,
A stunning castle is where you must go."

"It's got to mean the Snow Chateau," said Jasmine.

"Oh, I can't wait to see Lady Felicity again!" said Summer.

"And to be bridesmaids!" said Ellie in excitement. "Come on!"

They all touched the sides of the Magic Box. "The Snow Chateau!" they said.

There was a flash of green light and Trixi shot out of the box on her leaf.

"Yippee! You guessed that riddle quickly, girls!"

"Well, we knew where the wedding is happening, which helped," said Jasmine with a grin.

Trixi hovered between them on her leaf. She looked very smart in a green silk dress and a matching hat.

"Is everything OK at the chateau?" Summer asked.

"Everything is just fine," said Trixi happily. "The food has been prepared, the wedding cake looks amazing, the decorations are almost up, and the band

have just arrived. Are you ready to come
and be Lady Felicity's bridesmaids?"

"Oh yes!" said Ellie. "We couldn't be
more ready!"

Trixi tapped her ring as the girls held
hands:

"Take us into the north, to the wedding,
To meet Lady Felicity, Prince Noel and
the king."

Golden and silver confetti burst out of
her ring and surrounded the girls, swirling
around them and carrying them away.
Jasmine was glad no time ever passed
in the real world when they were in the
Secret Kingdom. Nani would have been
very surprised to come back downstairs
and find they had gone!

The girls landed on the steps of
a beautiful white castle that was
surrounded by snow-covered meadows.
Golden flags flew from the turrets, each
one embroidered with a giant silver
snowflake. The doors were open, and elf
butlers were bustling in and out, carrying
bunches of pink-and-white flowers.

The girls stepped inside
and found themselves
in a large hall
with a roaring
fire in a massive
fireplace. There
was a sweeping
staircase – the
bannister had
been decorated
with flowers and

twinkle-twinkle bunting was hung
around the walls. In the distance, the girls
could hear the sound of a band tuning
their instruments.

Jasmine felt excitement bubble up inside her. "Will there be dancing later on?"

"Oh yes, lots of dancing," said Trixi.

A man dressed in a smart gold suit came down the stairs. He was tall with pale blonde hair and kind blue eyes. His face lit up when he saw the girls and Trixi. "You must be Ellie, Summer and Jasmine," he said, sweeping into a deep bow. "Welcome to  my home. I am Prince Noel. My bride told me all about how you helped her yesterday. I am very grateful."

"It was our pleasure," said Jasmine.

"Lady Felicity and I are delighted that you have agreed to be her bridesmaids. Let me show you to her dressing room and she can give you your dresses."

The girls exchanged excited looks and followed him up the grand staircase.

Lady Felicity's dressing room was on the first floor.

"I shall leave you here," said Prince Noel, stopping by a door. "It would be bad luck to see Lady Felicity before the wedding. Now I must go with the carriages to meet the guests and bring them here. I shall see you at the wedding!"

He hurried off.

Ellie tapped on the door. "Lady Felicity? It's Ellie, Summer, Jasmine and Trixi."

"Come in!" called Lady Felicity. "I'm just having my hair done."

The girls opened the door and went into Lady Felicity's beautiful dressing room. A huge curved window with floaty lace curtains looked out across the palace gardens. Lady Felicity was sitting at a dressing table. Her dark hair had been swept up and secured with the ice mermaids' comb. An elf hairdresser was arranging tiny silver flowers in her hair-do.

Lady Felicity smiled at them. "I'm so glad you're here. Now we can have fun getting ready together. What do you think of my wedding dress?" She pointed to a dressmaker's dummy wearing it.

The girls all caught their breath. It was stunningly beautiful. The gown's bodice sparkled with diamonds and the full skirt was embroidered with silver snowflakes.

"I love it!" breathed Jasmine.

Lady Felicity looked pleased. "It's gorgeous,

isn't it? And wait until you see my cape."
She turned to the hairdresser. "Are you
finished yet, Sylvie?"

"All done, your ladyship," said the elf,
fixing the last silver flower in place.

"Thank you." Lady Felicity rose and
went to the big wardrobe at the side of
the room. She was about to open it when
she was interrupted by a knock on the
door.

Sylvie the hairdresser
opened it. An elf butler
was standing there
holding a silver tray.
On it was a present
wrapped in pink
tissue paper with
silver ribbons.

"This just arrived

for your ladyship," the butler said. "There was a note asking that it be brought to you straight away." He handed a note to Lady Felicity.

She read it out. "A very special gift to wear on your wedding day from a secret admirer." She blushed. "It must be from Prince Noel." She took the present from the tray. The butler and hairdresser left. "I wonder what it is," said Lady Felicity.

The girls and Trixi gathered round as Lady Felicity unwrapped the package. Inside was a beautiful white lace veil trimmed with pearls. "Oh," she exclaimed, putting her hand to her heart. "Noel must have chosen this for me to wear today. Isn't that romantic?"

The girls nodded.

"It really is," said Summer.

"It's beautiful," said Trixi.

Lady Felicity went to the mirror and attached the veil to the comb from the Ice Mermaids. She arranged it around her shoulders. "There. Isn't it—" She broke off with a cry of alarm as dark streaks appeared across the veil, turning the pretty lace flowers into ugly black spiders.

"What's going on?" Lady Felicity cried. "Help me, girls!"

Jasmine, Summer and Ellie all tried to take the veil off. They pulled and tugged, but it wouldn't budge. The veil was stuck to Lady Felicity's head!

A Cursed Wedding

BANG!

There was a crash of thunder. Lady Felicity screamed and the girls all gasped as Queen Malice suddenly appeared. She cackled in delight.

"Do you like your new veil?" she jeered, pointing at Lady Felicity. "It's a present from me!"

"You gave me this?" said Lady Felicity, holding up the blackened edges of the veil. "I thought it was from Prince Noel."

"I tricked you!" gloated the queen. "I'm not really a secret admirer. That veil is cursed. If you get married wearing it, your wedding day won't be the happiest day of your life – it will be the UNHAPPIEST!

Ha!" She shrieked with laughter and banged her thunderstaff on the floor. There was a flash of lightning and she disappeared, her nasty laughter echoing round the room.

"What am I going to do?" cried Lady Felicity, bursting into tears.

The girls rushed to comfort her.

"Queen Malice isn't going to get away with this," said Jasmine. "Don't worry, Lady Felicity."

"There must be a way to break the curse," said Ellie.

"Why is Queen Malice doing this?" wailed Lady Felicity.

"Because she doesn't want you and Prince Noel to get married," Trixi explained. "She knows it will fill the Secret Kingdom with love and magic."

Lady Felicity buried her head in her hands. "That's so mean."

Summer patted her on the back. "We'll do everything we can to help you."

From downstairs, they suddenly heard the muffled sound of crashes and shouts.

"Oh dear, that doesn't sound good," said Ellie.

"I wonder what's going on," said Jasmine, her heart racing. "Stay here, Lady Felicity. We'll be back as soon as we can."

They ran down the wide staircase.

"The noises seem to be coming from the kitchen!" called Trixi, zooming next to them on her leaf.

As they reached the kitchen door, the girls heard shrill voices that made their hearts sink.

"Squash the biscuits!"

"Mush the sandwiches!"

"Stamp on the jelly!"

"Oh no," Ellie said, looking at the others. "It's…"

"Storm Sprites!" Jasmine finished angrily.

They burst into the kitchen. Four bat-

like Storm Sprites – Queen Malice's
horrible servants – were flapping around,
attacking the platters of food the elves
had lovingly prepared. They were
throwing food at the walls with their
long, pointed fingers.

"You!" they shrieked, seeing the
girls. "Go away! We're going to

ruin the wedding!"

"You're the ones that should go away,"
shouted Jasmine. "Look at the mess you're
making!"

"We like mess!" cried one sprite. "We're
going to wreck the day for everyone."

"We hate weddings!" said another.
"Horrid lovey-dovey things."

"Down with weddings," they all
screeched.

They grabbed more handfuls of food
and threw them around the room.

Trixi touched her ring. But before
she could say a spell, a flying meringue
knocked her straight into a bowl of jelly.

The sprites cackled with delight.
"Look at the silly pixie! She's a jelly
pixie now!"

Luckily Trixi wasn't hurt but when

she climbed out of the jelly, her lovely
wedding clothes were ruined.

"Get the girls!" shouted the sprites.
Jasmine saw one of them reaching for the
wedding cake. It had three tiers and was
covered with white icing and pink sugar
roses.

"Oh, no you don't!" she yelled, running
towards him.

"Oh, yes I do!"
he shouted
gleefully,
pulling the top
layer off and
throwing it
at her like a
frisbee.

She ducked
and it splatted

onto the floor. The other sprites joined in,
throwing cake everywhere.

Jasmine, Ellie, Summer and Trixi
crouched under the table.

"What should we do?" said Summer.

Jasmine peeped out and her eyes fell on
a nearby stand full of frying pans. "OK.
I've got an idea." She crawled over to
the stand and grabbed some frying pans.
"Take these," she whispered, passing them
to her friends. "This is what we do…"

A moment later, the girls erupted from
under the table, yelling and swinging the
frying pans like tennis racquets.

SPLAT!

SPLOOGE!

The food hit the saucepans, flying
straight back at the sprite who threw it.

"Yuck!" screamed a sprite, wiping

cake from his face.

"Get lost, you meanies!" shouted
Jasmine.

The sprites continued to throw food,
but the girls were determined. They
swung their frying pans at anything that
flew towards them.

"Take that!" shouted Ellie, as she

batted back a pie.

"And that!" said Summer, thwacking a sandwich.

Covered in food, the sprites had soon had enough. They flapped out of the kitchen door and away.

"Phew! They've gone!" panted Ellie.

Summer looked round the kitchen.

"But look at the mess."

The wedding cake had been destroyed, the platters of food were ruined, the walls were splatted with jelly, cream and cakes.

"We'll have to fix it," said Jasmine.

"Um, girls, what's that noise?" said Trixi anxiously.

Now the sounds of shouting and

crashing were coming from the ballroom.

"Oh, no!" groaned Jasmine. "It must be the Storm Sprites again."

"Quick!" said Ellie, running out of the kitchen.

A Clever Trick

The Storm Sprites were flapping around
the ballroom, pulling down the twinkle-
twinkle bunting, tearing up flowers with
their long fingers, and gobbling the sweets
that had been arranged in a beautiful
rainbow-shaped display. The brownie
musicians and the elf butlers were
shouting at them but the sprites took no
notice.

"Wreck the wedding!" they screeched.

Summer, Ellie and Jasmine stopped in the doorway. "This is dreadful. We're just chasing them from room to room," said Ellie.

"We have to get rid of them for good," said Summer.

"But how?" asked Jasmine.

"There must be something we can do. Can anyone think of something that sprites hate?" said Ellie.

"Something that will make them fly away?"

"Well, they hate pretty things," said Summer. "And laughter and happiness and…and…"

"Weddings," said Jasmine. "They seem to hate those most of all."

Ellie gasped. "That's it! I've got an idea!" She ran to a nearby table and pulled a bouquet of flowers out of a vase. Then she jumped out in front of a Storm Sprite. "Congratulations!" she called, throwing the flowers at him.

He caught them and looked at her in confusion. "What do you mean? What are these stinky flowers for?"

"Don't you know?" said Ellie, looking surprised. "If you catch a

wedding bouquet it means you're going
to get married soon yourself."

"No!" shrieked the sprite.

The other three sprites all started to
cackle. "You're getting married!" they
jeered.

"No, I'm not!" the first sprite said. He
threw the bouquet at another sprite.
"You're the one with the flowers! You're
getting married!"

"Yuk!" the sprite shrieked. "I don't
want them." He threw them hard at
another sprite.

Ellie grabbed one of the white
tablecloths and put it over her head like a
veil. "So, who's going to be my husband,
then?" she sang, approaching them.

The sprites started squabbling, pushing
and shoving each other.

"Ew! You can be her husband."

"No, you can!"

Jasmine and Summer grabbed tablecloths and joined in. "We need husbands too," Summer said sweetly. "If you stay here you're going to have to marry us."

"I can be a bridesmaid!" called Trixi from her leaf.

"Who's going to come and kiss me?" said Jasmine, pursing her lips.

"Ugh!" the sprites yelled.

"Come here, husband!" said Summer, pretending to try and grab one.

"Kissy-kissy!" said Ellie, advancing on the sprites.

Yelling in alarm, the sprites flew over their heads and zoomed out of the ballroom, with Ellie, Summer and Jasmine

chasing them through the open front
door. They flapped away, glancing behind
them every so often with panicked looks
on their faces.

When the sprites had vanished from
view, Jasmine, Summer and Ellie burst out
laughing.

"Did you see their faces when you said you wanted a kiss, Jasmine?" hooted Summer.

"They looked terrified!" said Ellie, wiping tears of laughter from her eyes.

"That was a brilliant idea, Ellie," said Trixi.

Ellie chuckled. "I saw the flowers and it just popped into my head."

"Well, it got rid of them," said Jasmine.

"Now we've just got to deal with this mess," said Summer.

They looked round the ballroom. All the decorations were ruined, the chairs and musical instruments had been knocked over and the sweets had been eaten.

"How can we possibly make everything

look lovely again?" said Ellie. "Prince Noel will be arriving with the guests soon."

"We'll never be able to clear the mess up in time," said Trixi. "And what about the food? The sprites have ruined it all."

"There's not even a wedding cake," said Jasmine.

"OK, first things first," said Summer. "If we can't tidy this room up in time, could the wedding take place somewhere else?"

"There are no other rooms big enough," said Trixi.

Jasmine looked out at the snowy garden. "What about outdoors? My Nani got married outside. Maybe the prince and Lady Felicity could hold the wedding out there."

"Won't it be too cold?" said Ellie.

"Maybe not," said Trixi. "Go outside."

The girls ran out on to the snowy lawn. Even though snow covered the grass and sparkling icicles hung from the trees' branches, the air didn't feel cold. It felt like a mild spring day.

"It's warm out here," said Jasmine in surprise.

Trixi smiled. "That's because of all the love warming the air. We could bring the chairs and tables and instruments out here and set up an area where Prince Noel and Lady Felicity can get married.

If we hurry, we'll get it done before the guests arrive."

Trixi flew back inside and explained what needed to be done. The brownies and elves helped them carry the tables, chairs and musical instruments outside. The butlers hung twinkle-twinkle bunting up on the trees while the girls set the tables. Trixi used her magic ring to conjure up an arched trellis covered with flowers and a big, white silk tent with pink bows.

"There – finished!" said Trixi in relief. She sat down on her leaf, looking very pale.

"Are you OK?" Summer said.

Trixi nodded. "Yes. I used quite a lot of magic to conjure all that up. I'm feeling tired now."

"We still need to do something about the food and the cake," said Jasmine.

Trixi looked anxious. "There isn't enough time for the elves to make everything again. I'm going to have to use more magic."

"You don't look very well," said Summer. "Are you sure you should?"

"I'll have to try," said Trixi bravely. "We can't have a wedding without food." She took a deep breath and called out wearily:

"Pixie magic, please grant my requests,
Bring food and drink for the
wedding guests."

She tapped her ring. There was a bright flash and suddenly the tables were filled with wobbly jellies in all colours of the rainbow, tiny sandwiches, iced biscuits, little meringues and pretty pastel macaroons.

"You did it, Trixi!" cried Jasmine in delight.

Trixi put her hand to her forehead. "I don't feel very well. I think I'm going to…"

Her eyes shut and she fainted.

Wedding Cake Rescue

"Trixi!" the girls gasped.

Summer gently stroked the pixie's
back.

Trixi's blue eyes fluttered open and
she sat up. "I'm sorry," she said dazedly.
"I'm fine. Really, I am. I'm just a bit
tired. I'll sort the wedding cake out in a
moment."

"No. You're not going to do any more magic," Jasmine said firmly. "You need to rest now."

"Jasmine's right," said Summer. "The cake isn't important. We can have the wedding without it."

"What?" A loud, cheerful voice made them swing round. "Have a wedding without a cake? Not when I'm here!"

"Mrs Sherbet!" gasped the girls. They had met Mrs Sherbet when they had gone to Candy Cove. She was a round, cheerful lady who had a magic sweetshop that travelled all over the Secret Kingdom.

She bustled over, a giant pink-and-white candy cane tucked under her arm. "Now, what's all this about no cake, girls?"

"It's the wedding cake," explained
Summer. "The Storm Sprites
destroyed it."

Mrs Sherbet
beamed. "Then isn't
it lucky I arrived
early? Show me
what's left of
the cake and I'll
see if my candy
cane can work its
magic."

The girls knew that
whenever Mrs Sherbet's candy cane
touched a sweet treat, more appeared.

"The cake's in the kitchen, Mrs
Sherbet," said Summer. She gently picked
up Trixi and her leaf and led everyone
into the kitchen.

Inside, the elves were clearing up, wiping the walls and sweeping the floors.

"What are we going to do?" an elf said. "The cake is ruined."

The top two layers of the wedding cake were squashed on the floor. Only the bottom later was still on its silver stand.

"Never fear, Mrs Sherbet is here!" She went over to the cake and inspected what was left. "Yes, yes. I think we can soon sort this out. Tell me – what sort of cake do you think Lady Felicity would like?"

"Chocolate cake," said Jasmine.

"With lots of icing and pink flowers," said Ellie.

"And with a bride and groom on top," added Summer.

"Very well. Here we go!" Mrs Sherbet lifted her candy cane and touched it to the remaining cake.

FLASH!

Bright pink light lit up the room and the girls gasped. A beautiful wedding cake was balancing on the stand. It had five layers, all covered with sparkling snow-white icing and scattered with

pink sugar flowers. It was topped with a
marzipan bride and groom who looked
just like Lady
Felicity and
Prince Noel.

"There!"
said Mrs
Sherbet
with a
satisfied
sigh as the
elves and
girls clapped
in delight.

"Amazing!" said
Jasmine.

"It looks delicious!" said Ellie.

"Lady Felicity will love it," said
Summer.

"Now, let me conjure up some extra sweets," said Mrs Sherbet. "There should always be lots of sweets at a wedding."

"That would be brilliant," said Summer. "The Storm Sprites ate all the sweets in the ballroom."

"While you do that, we'll go and check on Lady Felicity," said Jasmine.

"That's fine, my dears!" Mrs Sherbet sailed out of the kitchen. "I shall see you at the wedding."

"If there is a wedding," said Ellie in a low voice. "I don't see how Lady Felicity can get married in that horrible veil."

They hurried upstairs, taking Trixi with them.

Ellie knocked on Lady Felicity's dressing room door. "Lady Felicity?"

"Come in!" called Lady Felicity.

They opened the door and caught their breath. Lady Felicity had changed into her wedding dress. Despite the horrid black veil, she looked stunning.

Over the beautiful dress she wore a long cape with a fur collar. The fairy goldsmiths' diamond necklace sparkled around her neck.

"Oh, Lady Felicity, you look gorgeous," said Summer.

"I hope Prince Noel thinks so too when I walk down the aisle," said Lady Felicity, with a smile.

"But what about Queen Malice's veil?" asked Jasmine.

"It doesn't matter," said Lady Felicity. "I've been watching you all through the window. I realised I can't let Queen Malice spoil my wedding. Prince Noel and I love each other and we'll make sure our special day is full of love and happiness, no matter what Malice's stupid curse says."

As she spoke, there was a loud rumble of thunder that made everything in the chateau shake.

Queen Malice appeared in the dressing room again. The girls rushed to stand protectively in front of Lady Felicity.

"So, you thought you'd fix things, did you?" Queen Malice hissed, pointing her thunderstaff at the girls. "Well, think again!"

Beautiful Bridesmaids

"Go away," Queen Malice!" said Jasmine, stepping towards her bravely. "The wedding is going ahead whether you like it or not."

"Everything will go wrong," snarled the queen. "I'll cause chaos, I'll make the decorations fall down again, I'll ruin the food, I'll silence the music…"

"So what?" Ellie interrupted. "Those things don't matter. Food, music, a wedding cake – they're lovely but they're not what's important."

Summer nodded. "All that matters is that Lady Felicity and Prince Noel love each other."

"And their family and friends love them too," said Jasmine.

"The girls are right," said Lady Felicity, putting her hands on her hips. "Love really is the only thing that matters!"

There was a bright flash and suddenly the veil started changing from black to white.

Queen Malice screamed in fury. "No!"

But it was too late. Lady Felicity's words had broken the curse! Sparkling light swirled round the room, filling the girls with warmth and happiness. As it passed over Trixi, the colour returned to her face and she jumped to her feet, her magic renewed. The light spread through the rest of the chateau and across the garden, making everything it touched sparkle.

"Gah!" cried Queen Malice, brushing furiously at her dark cloak and dress. "I'm covered in glitter!"

"Isn't it wonderful?" said Lady Felicity, beaming. "Now, you're very welcome to stay for the wedding, Queen Malice. I wouldn't like you to feel left out. But there will be lots more glitter and plenty of love and laughter…"

With a scream of disgust, the queen thumped her thunderstaff on the ground and disappeared, howling, "Noooooooooo!"

As her scream faded, the girls burst out laughing.

"Oh, dear. Queen Malice didn't like the sound of that," said Jasmine.

"I do," said Summer, grinning.

"I feel completely back to normal now!" Trixi said, turning a loop-the-loop on her leaf.

She whizzed to a stop in front of the window. "Oh, my goodness, all the guests are arriving. Look!"

The others rushed to the window. Prince Noel and the elf butlers were showing people to their seats. King Merry had arrived and was sitting on a throne, waiting to conduct the ceremony. He was dressed in a red suit with white trim looking like a small, round Father Christmas.

"It's almost time for the wedding to start," said Lady Felicity, straightening her snowy white veil.

"But what about the girls?" said Trixi. "They haven't got their bridesmaid dresses on."

"I think a little magic is called for," said Lady Felicity. "Are you feeling up to it, Trixi?"

"Oh, yes!" Trixi cried, tapping her ring.

There was a bright flash and the girls gasped. They were suddenly wearing the prettiest bridesmaid dresses imaginable, each holding a bouquet of flowers and a little basket filled with petals. Summer's white dress had pink flowers and butterflies embroidered around the hem, and she wore a matching fur cape

that tied with a bow. Jasmine's dress had
a lilac skirt with a little pink fur jacket
on top. Ellie's had a white jacket and her
swirly dress was a lovely shade of pink.

"Oh, wow!" said Jasmine, doing a
twirl.

"I love my dress!" said Ellie, running to the mirror.

"And I love mine too," said Summer.

"You all look beautiful," said Trixi in delight.

"But what about you, Trixi?" said Jasmine.

Trixi's wedding outfit was ruined from falling into the jelly.

"Oh, I think I can help Trixi," said Lady Felicity. "After all, she's not the only one with a magic pixie ring." She took a ring off her dressing table. It was the gold band with pink hearts that Trixi's Aunt Maybelle had given the girls.

"Now, let me see…" Lady Felicity tapped it and whispered a few words.

There was another bright flash and suddenly Trixi was wearing a new outfit too! It was a green dress made of silk pixie leaves. She had a little white fur cape tied with a green ribbon and a crown of dark pink blossoms on her head. In her hands she held a bouquet of matching pink flowers.

"Oh goodness!" she cried, looking down at her dress. "Thank you, Lady Felicity!"

"You look beautiful. Would you do me the honour of being my ring-bearer?" said Lady Felicity.

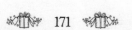

"I'd love to!" said
Trixi in delight.
Lady Felicity
handed her
the ring and
Trixi placed
it carefully
on her
leaf, which
was also
decorated
with pink
flowers.

Jasmine went to the
window. "The music's starting."

"Then we should go downstairs," said
Lady Felicity. "I don't want to keep
Prince Noel waiting!" She straightened
the mermaids' comb in her hair, picked

up the gold horseshoe from her dressing
table and beamed at the girls. "It's time
for this wedding to begin!"

Here Comes the Bride

In the garden, Prince Noel was waiting under the trellis with King Merry. The seats were filled with lots of familiar, smiling faces. Mrs Sherbet was sitting in between two groups of brownies – one from the Sugarsweet Bakery and one from Fairytale Forest. Clara Columbus, a pixie explorer, was chatting to

Winterberry, the brownie who ran the snow bear sanctuary. Next to them sat Gena, a genie from the Silver Desert, Jasper Rococo, the kingdom's most famous artist, and the elegant Swan Queen.

Some of the guests didn't need seats.

Aunt Maybelle and a troop of pixies
were hovering on their leaves, while
fairies from the Snowy Slopes and
Glitter Beach fluttered around them.
Swift and a few other flying horses stood
next to Littlehorn and a small group of
unicorns.

The brownie musicians blew a fanfare on their trumpets. Everyone turned round and as they saw Lady Felicity, they burst into a chorus oohs and ahhs. Prince Noel smiled and held out his hand to her. The band began to play a wedding march and Lady Felicity walked slowly down the aisle, a happy smile on her face.

Trixi flew in front of the bride, scattering petals and Ellie, Summer and

Jasmine walked behind, carefully carrying the train of Lady Felicity's dress. King Merry looked like he was going to pop with delight.

When Lady Felicity reached Prince Noel, the music stopped and King Merry cleared his throat.

"Dearest friends, we are gathered here today to witness the wedding of my cousin, Lady Felicity, to Prince Noel. Please down sit…I mean sit down," he hastily corrected himself. "And the begin will wedding. Oh dear, I mean and the wedding will begin." He blushed. "I'm a bit overcome. I love weddings! Now, where were we? Ah yes, I need the ring." He started patting his pockets anxiously. "The ring. Oh dearie me. Whatever have I done with the ring?"

Trixi flew over and held out the ring. "It's all right, King Merry. I've got it!"

The king looked very relieved. "Thank you, Trixi, I don't

know what I'd do without you."

"You're doing just fine, your majesty," said Trixi. The girls saw her secretly tap her ring and whisper something as she flew to the side.

A look of confidence settled over King Merry. "Let's begin with the wedding vows," he said calmly. "Lady Felicity, if you would repeat after me…"

King Merry didn't make another mistake. The wedding went perfectly. Lady Felicity and Prince Noel promised to love and make each other happy for the rest of their lives. Then Prince Noel slipped the ring on to Lady Felicity's finger.

"I now pronounce you husband and wife!" said King Merry. "You may kiss the bride."

Prince Noel swept Lady Felicity into a kiss. Sparkly magical snowflakes started drifting down from the sky, even though the sun was still shining. Everyone cheered and then the gnomes from King Merry's secret garden shook white bell-shaped flowers that rang out joyfully. As the bride and groom walked back up the aisle, the pixies flew high above holding a banner that read: CONGRATULATIONS.

Then, the wedding turned into a party. The elf butlers gave out glasses of starflower fizz and handed round silver platters piled with the delicious treats that Trixi had conjured up. As they ate and drank, Summer, Jasmine and Ellie had fun catching up with old friends.

Overhead, the pixies performed a

daring routine of flips and spins that
made the audience gasp. After that, Lady
Felicity and Prince Noel cut the wedding
cake together. Soon everyone was
dancing – even the unicorns and flying
horses!

Ellie, Summer and Jasmine danced
together first of all and then with King
Merry, who kept tripping over his feet.
Next, Prince Noel danced with each of
them. He swept them round and round
the garden. With her beautiful dress on,
Summer almost felt like a fairy-tale bride
herself!

Gradually, shadows lengthened and the
sun began to set.

"It's time for us to go on our
honeymoon!" the prince announced to
the crowd.

He held out his hand and Lady Felicity
ran to his side, her eyes sparkling.

"It's been the most wonderful wedding,"
she said. "Thank you all for coming.
Thank you to King Merry for leading
the ceremony and to Trixi for conjuring

up all the things we needed. Thank you
all for your help and your amazing gifts.
We will come and visit everyone soon.
Most of all –" her eyes fell on Ellie,
Summer and Jasmine "– thank you to
three very special friends. Without them,
there would have been no wedding." She
blew kisses to them all.

Everyone clapped loudly. The girls blushed in delight.

"We're so happy we could help," said Jasmine.

"We've loved being bridesmaids," said Summer.

"Three cheers for Lady Felicity and Prince Noel!" called Ellie. "Hip, hip... hooray!"

The guests cheered so loudly that snow fell off the branches of the trees. As the applause faded there was the sound of ringing bells and four silver reindeer

pulled a golden sleigh into the garden.
Prince Noel helped Lady Felicity in,
then he took the reins and the reindeer
pranced off across the snow.

At the last moment, Lady Felicity threw
her bouquet. It arched towards the guests.

It flew over the girls'
heads and then Mrs
Sherbet caught it!

She whooped
with delight.
"Butterscotch
and bonbons!
I've got the
bouquet!"
She grabbed
King Merry and
waltzed round with him,
chuckling.

"Maybe there will be another Secret
Kingdom wedding soon!" Ellie whispered
to the others.

They all giggled.

When he'd finished dancing, King
Merry came over to the girls with Trixi

flying beside him. "My dears, what can I say?" he said. "You saved the day yet again."

"It wasn't just us," said Jasmine. "Lots of other people helped."

"I think the wedding showed what's best about the Secret Kingdom," said Summer. "When everyone works together, anything is possible."

"What makes the Secret Kingdom so special isn't just the magic, it's all the love and kindness everyone shows to each other," said Ellie.

"Well, everyone apart from Queen Malice and the Storm Sprites," said Jasmine with a grin.

"Oh dear, my dreadful sister," sighed King Merry, shaking his head. "I hope she doesn't start causing trouble again."

"Well, if she does, just let us know," said Ellie. "We'll be back here in a flash!"

"And if she doesn't, we're happy to visit just for fun!" said Summer.

"We always love coming to the Secret Kingdom," said Jasmine.

They all hugged the king.

Trixi kissed each of the girls on the nose with a feather-light kiss. "See you soon for another adventure," she told them.

She tapped her ring. Silver confetti whooshed out and swirled around the girls. They felt themselves being carried away back to Jasmine's house.

"Oh, wow! That was the best adventure yet!" said Jasmine, her eyes shining.

"I loved the wedding," said Ellie. "All those gorgeous clothes!" She saw a pen and some scrap paper on the coffee table and started to draw a wedding dress. "This is what I'd wear if I got married."

Jasmine put the Magic Box back in her bag and then twirled around the room. "If I had a wedding, I'd dance all night."

"I'd arrive in a horse-drawn carriage,"
said Summer. "And invite lots of
animals."

Just then, Nani came back in holding a bag full of colourful saris. "Still talking about weddings, girls? Well, you know something? The most important thing to have at a wedding is love."

The girls smiled at each other. "We know," they said.

If you love

Secret Kingdom

**you'll love Rosie Banks'
brand-new series,
Wish Princesses!**

Charlotte and Mia are best friends,
but Charlotte's family are moving to
America, and the girls will never see
each other. Until they discover the
magic of the Wish Princesses!

As the girls work to become
Wish Princesses they have lots
of magical adventures

– and best of all,
they can see each other
whenever they want!

Read on for a sneak peek...

"I've got a present for you," said
Mia. Charlotte sat down on the
bottom bunk while Mia fetched a
large scrapbook then sat beside her. The
scrapbook had a pink cover and she
had written the words Best Friends Are
Forever on the front. "I made this for
you," she said, shyly. "I hope you
like it."

Charlotte opened it. It was
full of photos of them both.
They started when they
were babies lying on a

playmat together,
then when they were
toddlers dressed as princesses
and then on their first day at
school when they were wearing
uniforms that looked much too big
and both had their hair in funny
sticking-out bunches.

"Oh, wow," she said, turning the pages.
"This is awesome. I love it!" Mia had also
stuck in some special things amongst the
photos – a birthday card Charlotte had
sent her when she was five; a rule
book from the friendship club they
had made up together; a ticket stub
from a concert that they had
gone to last year. Charlotte
bit her lip, feeling happy and
sad at the same time.

"Thank you. I'll keep it forever."

"Which is how long we'll be friends for," said Mia.

They hugged each other. "I don't want to go," whispered Charlotte, her eyes stinging with tears.

"I don't want you to either," said Mia bravely. "But we'll always be best friends. No matter how far apart we are."

"Always," promised Charlotte.

As they hugged, there was a knock at the door. The girls looked at each other in surprise. Who could it be?

"Come in!" called Charlotte. A beautiful older girl with strawberry blonde hair streaked with bright red opened the door. She was wearing a short denim skirt and sparkly sandals. On her white crop top rested a familiar necklace shaped like a musical note, so shiny that it almost seemed to glow.

"Alice!" Charlotte and Mia gasped, jumping to their feet. It was always so amazing to think that their old babysitter, Alice, was now a pop star!

Their pop star friend looked incredibly glamorous, but her smile was just as warm as ever. "Your mums are looking for you. I thought I might find you here."

They ran over and hugged her. "How come you're back?" Mia said.

"Your mum emailed me about the party and I really wanted to come. I'm only here for a few hours, though. I have to travel up north for a concert I'm doing tomorrow night, but I couldn't let Charlotte go to California without saying goodbye," said Alice. "I can't believe you're moving."

"I know," said Charlotte.

They all sat down on the bed together. Despite feeling miserable about leaving, Charlotte couldn't help but smile as she looked at Alice. It was so nice to see her again. "I'm so glad you could come."

Alice squeezed her hand. "So why aren't you

two downstairs dancing?"

Mia swallowed. "We didn't feel like it."

Alice's blue eyes softened. "I know it's hard, but you can still be best friends even if you're far apart."

"It's just not going to be the same," said Charlotte, sighing. "We won't be able to see each other much."

Alice looked from one girl to the other. "Maybe you will."

"What do you mean?" said Charlotte.

Alice smiled mysteriously and pulled something out of her pocket. It was a silver necklace. "Charlotte and Mia," she murmured. She closed

her hand for a
moment.

When Alice opened her
hand again, there were two
silver necklaces nestled in her
palm!

"How…how did you do that?"
stammered Mia, astonished.

Alice jumped to her feet. "There isn't
time to explain right now. Just remember
this…" She handed them each a
necklace. "Wishes do come true. As long
as you keep each other in your hearts,
you'll never be alone. Now quick –
put the necklaces on."

Charlotte fastened the necklace
she was holding around Mia's
neck, then Mia did the
same for her.

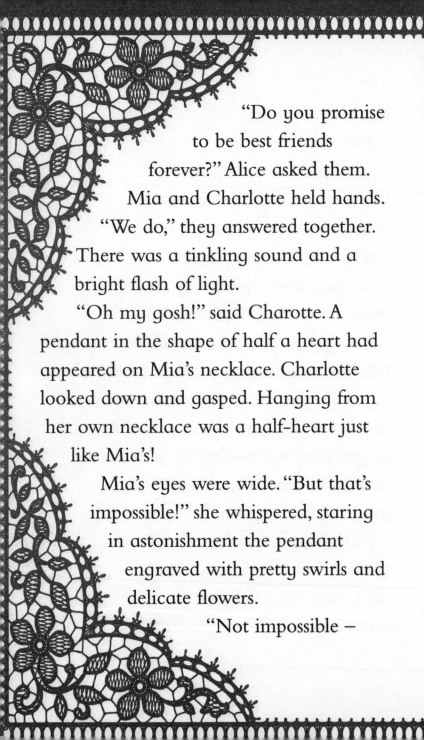

"Do you promise
to be best friends
forever?" Alice asked them.
Mia and Charlotte held hands.
"We do," they answered together.
There was a tinkling sound and a
bright flash of light.

"Oh my gosh!" said Charotte. A
pendant in the shape of half a heart had
appeared on Mia's necklace. Charlotte
looked down and gasped. Hanging from
her own necklace was a half-heart just
like Mia's!

Mia's eyes were wide. "But that's
impossible!" she whispered, staring
in astonishment the pendant
engraved with pretty swirls and
delicate flowers.

"Not impossible –

magic!" Alice said
softly before kissing
them each on the cheek. "I
just knew you'd be special," she
said mysteriously.

Mia gently lifted her pendant and
held it against Charlotte's. Together,
they formed a perfect heart. Mia's
hand tingled as the heart began to glow,
filling her bedroom with warm, bright
light. She was so excited she could barely
breathe.

Read Wish Princesses:
Forever Friends to find out
what happens next!

Secret Kingdom

Keep all your dreams and wishes safe in this gorgeous Secret Kingdom Notebook!

Includes a party planner, diary, dream journal and lots more!

Out now!

Competition!

Would you like to win a Secret Kingdom goody bag?

All you have to do is read the story and tell us:

Who makes the replacement golden horseshoe for Lady Felicity?

When you think you have the answer, go online to

www.secretkingdombooks.com

and click on the competition to enter your details.

We will put all the correct entries into a draw and select three winners to receive this special gift.

Good luck!

Closing date: 31st March 2016

Collect all the amazing Secret Kingdom specials - with two exciting adventures in one!

Christmas Castle

ROSIE BANKS

Dolphin Bay

ROSIE BANKS

Christmas Ballerina

ROSIE BANKS

Pixie Princess

ROSIE BANKS

Starlight Adventure

ROSIE BANKS

Candy Cove Pirates

ROSIE BANKS

Code Maze!

Trixi is stuck!

Can you help her get through the Secret Kingdom maze?

Use the key to guide Trixi to Ellie, Summer and Jasmine

Key

 = Right   = Up   = Left   = Down

Secret Kingdom

A magical world of
friendship and fun!

Join the Secret Kingdom Club at

www.secretkingdombooks.com

and enjoy games, sneak peeks and lots more!

You'll find great activities, competitions, stories
and games, plus a special newsletter for
Secret Kingdom friends!